Dr. August Forel

Ants and Some Other Insects

GW00541768

outlook

Dr. August Forel

Ants and Some Other Insects

1st Edition | ISBN: 978-3-75234-843-9

Place of Publication: Frankfurt am Main, Germany

Year of Publication: 2020

Outlook Verlag GmbH, Germany.

Reproduction of the original.

Ants and Some Other Insects

By
Dr. August Forel

1

W HEN discussing the ant-mind, we must consider that these small animals, on the one hand, differ very widely from ourselves in organisation, but on the other hand, have come, through so-called convergence, to possess in the form of a social commonwealth a peculiar relationship to us. My subject, however, requires the discussion of so many complicated questions that I am compelled to assume acquaintance with the work of others, especially the elements of psychology, and in addition the works of P. Huber, Wasmann, von Buttel-Reepen, Darwin, Romanes, Lubbock, my *Fourmis de la Suisse*, and many others. Since the functions of the sense-organs constitute the basis of comparative psychology, I must also refer to a series of articles entitled "Sensations des Insectes" which I have recently published (1900-1901) in the *Rivista de Biologia Generale*, edited by Dr. P. Celesia. In these papers I have defined my position with respect to various authors, especially Plateau and Bethe.

Very recently Bethe, Uexkull, and others have denied the existence of psychic powers in invertebrate animals. They explain the latter as reflex-machines, and take their stand on the ground of the so-called psycho-physical parallelism for the purpose of demonstrating our inability to recognise mental qualities in these animals. They believe, however, that they can prove the mechanical regularity of behavior, but assume unknown forces whenever they are left in the lurch in their explanations. They regard the mind as first making its appearance in the vertebrates, whereas the old Cartesians regarded all animals, in contradistinction to man, as mindless (unconscious) machines.

The Jesuit father E. Wasmann and von Buttel-Reepen are willing, on the other hand, to accept the inductive inference from analogy as a valid scientific method. Like Lubbock, the lecturer and others, they advocate a comparative psychology of the invertebrates and convincingly demonstrate the existence of psychic faculties in these animals. Wasmann, however, puts a very low estimate on the mental powers of the higher vertebrates and, in my opinion, improperly, denies to them any ability of drawing inferences from experience when in the presence of new conditions (this alone he designates as intelligence); he believes that man alone possesses an immortal soul (independent of natural laws?) in addition to the animal mind.

It is necessary, first of all, to arrive at some common understanding concerning the obscure notion "psychic" in order that we may avoid logomachy, and carrying on theology in the sense of Goethe's Mephistopheles. Two concepts are confounded in an obscure manner in the word "psychic": first, the abstract concept of introspection, or subjectivism, i. e., observation from within, which every person knows only, and can know only, in and by himself. For this let us reserve the term "consciousness." Second, the "activity" of the mind or that which determines the contents of the field of consciousness. This has been included without further ado with consciousness in the wider sense, and thence has arisen the confusion of regarding consciousness as an attribute of the mind. In another place I have designated the molecular wave of activity of the neural elements as "neurocyme."

We cannot speak of the consciousness of human beings other than ourselves without drawing an inference from analogy; quite as little ought we to speak of a consciousness of forgotten things. The field of our consciousness is constantly changing. Things appear in it and disappear from it. Memory, through association, enables us to recall, more or less directly and with more or less difficulty, things which appear to be momentarily absent from consciousness. Moreover, both the experience of self-observation and the phenomena of hypnotism teach us experimentally that many things of which we seem to be unconscious, are nevertheless present in consciousness or have been. Indeed, certain sense-impressions remain, at the moment of their occurrence, unconscious so far as our ordinary consciousness or superconsciousness is concerned, although they can be subsequently recalled into consciousness by suggestion. Whole chains of brain-activities, (dreams, somnambulism, or secondary consciousness) seem ordinarily to be excluded from the superconsciousness, but may subsequently be associated by suggestion with the remembered contents of consciousness. In all these cases, therefore, what seems to be unconscious is after all proved to be conscious. The above-mentioned phenomena have frequently led to mystical interpretations, but they are explainable on a very simple assumption. Let us assume—and this is quite in harmony with observation—that the fields of the introspectively conscious brain-activities are limited by so-called association or dissociation processes, i. e., that we are unable actively to bring them all into connection at the same time, and that therefore all that seems to us unconscious has also in reality a consciousness, in other words, a subjective reflex, then the following results: Our ordinary waking consciousness or superconsciousness is merely an inner subjective reflex of those activities of attention which are most intimately connected with one another, i. e., of the more intensively concentrated maxima of our cerebral activities during waking. There exist, however, other consciousnesses, partly forgotten, partly only loosely or indirectly connected with the contents of the superconsciousness, in contradistinction to which these may be designated as subconsciousness. They correspond to other less concentrated or otherwise associated cerebral activities. We are bound to assume the existence of still more remotely interconnected subconsciousnesses for the infra-cortical (lower) brain-centers, and so on.

It is easy to establish the fact that the maximum of our psychic activity, namely, attention, passes every moment from one perception or thought to another. These objects of attention, as visual or auditory images, will-impulses, feelings or abstract thoughts, come into play—and of this there is no doubt—in different brain-regions or neuron-complexes. We can therefore compare attention to a functional *macula lutea* wandering in the brain, or with a wandering maximal intensity of neurocymic activity. But it is quite as satisfactorily established that other psychic phenomena external to attention are likewise present in consciousness, though in a feebler condition. Finally, it is well known that all that has been in consciousness—even that which is now more, now less, forgotten—is included in the psychic, i. e., in the contents of consciousness. On superficial consideration this appears to satisfy theoretical requirements. But in fact and in truth there are innumerable processes of which we are feebly conscious for only a scarcely appreciable instant and which anon disappear from consciousness. Here and not in the strong and repeated "psychomes"—I beg your indulgence for this word, with which I would for the sake of brevity designate each and every psychic unit—are we to seek the transition from the conscious to the apparently unconscious. Even in this case, however, the feeble condition of consciousness is only apparent, because the inner reflex of these processes can merely echo faintly in the field of a strongly diverted attention. This, therefore, in no wise proves that such half conscious processes are in and for themselves so feebly represented in consciousness, since a flash of attention is sufficient subsequently to give them definite shape in consciousness. Only in consequence of the diversion of the attention do they lose more and more their connection with the chain of intensity-maxima which, under ordinary circumstances, constitute the remembered contents of our superconsciousness. The more feebly, however, they are bound to the latter, with the more difficulty are such half-conscious processes later associated anew through memory with the dominant chain. Of such a nature are all dreams, all the subordinate circumstances of our lives, all automatised habits, all instincts. But if there exists between the clearly conscious and the unconscious, a half-conscious brain-life, whose consciousness appears to us so feeble merely on account of the deviation of our ordinary train of memories, this is an unequivocal indication that a step further on the remaining connection would be completely severed, so that we should no longer have the right to say that the brain-activities thus fading away nebulously from our superconsciousness do not have consciousness in and for themselves. For the sake of brevity and simplicity we will ascribe

4

subconsciousness to these so-called unconscious brain-processes.

If this assumption is correct—and all things point in this direction—we are not further concerned with consciousness. It does not at all exist as such, but only through the brain-activity of which it is the inner reflex. With the disappearance of this activity, consciousness disappears. When the one is complicated, the other, too, is complicated. When the one is simple, the other is correspondingly simple. If the brain-activity be dissociated, consciousness also becomes dissociated. Consciousness is only an abstract concept, which loses all its substance with the falling away of "conscious" brain-activity. The brain-activity reflected in the mirror of consciousness appears therein subjectively as a summary synthesis, and the synthetical summation grows with the higher complications and abstractions acquired through habit and practice, so that details previously conscious (e. g., those involved in the act of reading) later become subconscious, and the whole takes on the semblance of a psychical unit.

Psychology, therefore, cannot restrict itself merely to a study of the phenomena of our superconsciousness by means of introspection, for the science would be impossible under such circumstances. Everybody would have only his own subjective psychology, after the manner of the old scholastic spiritualists, and would therefore be compelled to doubt the very existence of the external world and his fellow-men. Inference from analogy, scientific induction, the comparison of the experiences of our five senses, prove to us the existence of the outer world, our fellow-men and the psychology of the latter. They also prove to us that there is such a thing as comparative psychology, a psychology of animals. Finally our own psychology, without reference to our brain-activity, is an incomprehensible patchwork full of contradictions, a patchwork which above all things seems to contradict the law of the conservation of energy.

It follows, furthermore, from these really very simple reflections that a psychology that would ignore brain-activity, is a monstrous impossibility. The contents of our superconsciousness are continually influenced and conditioned by subconscious brain-activities. Without these latter it can never be understood. On the other hand, we understand the full value and the ground of the complex organisation of our brain only when we observe it in the inner light of consciousness, and when this observation is supplemented by a comparison of the consciousness of our fellow-men as this is rendered possible for us through spoken and written language by means of very detailed inferences from analogy. The mind must therefore be studied simultaneously from within and from without. Outside ourselves the mind can, to be sure, be studied only through analogy, but we are compelled to make use of this the only method which we possess.

Some one has said that language was given to man not so much for the expression as for the concealment of his thoughts. It is also well known that different men in all honesty attribute very different meanings to the same words. A savant, an artist, a peasant, a woman, a wild Wedda from Ceylon, interpret the same words very differently. Even the same individual interprets them differently according to his moods and their context. Hence it follows that to the psychologist and especially to the psychiatrist—and as such I am here speaking—the mimetic expression, glances and acts of a man often betray his true inner being better than his spoken language. Hence also the attitudes and behavior of animals have for us the value of a "language," the psychological importance of which must not be underestimated. Moreover, the anatomy, physiology and pathology of the animal and human brain have yielded irrefutable proof that our mental faculties depend on the quality, quantity, and integrity of the living brain and are one with the same. It is just as impossible that there should exist a human brain without a mind, as a mind without a brain, and to every normal or pathological change in the mental activity, there corresponds a normal or pathological change of the neurocymic activity of the brain, i. e., of its nervous elements. Hence what we perceive introspectively in consciousness is cerebral activity.

As regards the relation of pure psychology (introspection) to the physiology of the brain (observation of brain-activity from without), we shall take the theory of identity for granted so long as it is in harmony with the facts. The word identity, or monism, implies that every psychic phenomenon is the same real thing as the molecular or neurocymic activity of the brain-cortex coinciding with it, but that this may be viewed from two standpoints. The phenomenon alone is dualistic, the thing itself is monistic. If this were otherwise there would result from the accession of the purely psychical to the physical, or cerebral, an excess of energy which would necessarily contradict the law of the conservation of energy. Such a contradiction, however, has never been demonstrated and would hold up to derision all scientific experience. In the manifestations of our brain-life, wonderful as they undoubtedly are, there is absolutely nothing which contradicts natural laws and justifies us in postulating the existence of a mythical, supernatural "psyche."

On this account I speak of monistic identity and not of psycho-physical parallelism. A thing cannot be parallel with itself. Of course, psychologists of the modern school, when they make use of this term, desire merely to designate a supposed parallelism of phenomena without prejudice either to monism or dualism. Since, however, many central nervous processes are accessible neither to physiological nor to psychological observation, the phenomena accessible to us through these two methods of investigation are not in the least parallel, but separated from one another very unequally by intermediate processes. Moreover, inasmuch as the dualistic hypothesis is scientifically untenable, it is altogether proper to start out from the hypothesis of identity.

It is as clear as day that the same activity in the nervous system of an animal, or even in my own nervous system, observed by myself, first by means of physiological methods from without, and second, as reflecting itself in my consciousness, must appear to me to be totally different, and it would indeed be labor lost to try to convert the physiological into psychological qualities or *vice versa*. We cannot even convert one psychological quality into another, so far as the reality symbolised by both is concerned; e. g., the tone, the visual and tactile sensation, which a uniform, low, tuning-fork vibration produces on our three corresponding senses. Nevertheless, we may infer inductively that it is the same reality, the same vibration which is symbolised for us in these three qualitatively and totally different modes i. e., produces in us these three different psychical impressions which cannot be transformed into one another. These impressions depend on activities in different parts of the brain and are, of course, as such actually different from one another in the brain. We speak of psycho-physiological identity only when we mean, on the one hand, the cortical neurocyme which directly conditions the conscious phenomena known to us, on the other hand, the corresponding phenomena of consciousness.

And, in fact, a mind conceived as dualistic could only be devoid of energy or energy-containing. If it be conceived as devoid of energy (Wasmann), i. e., independent of the laws of energy, we have arrived at a belief in the miraculous, a belief which countenances the interference with and arbitrary suspension of the laws of nature. If it be conceived as energy-containing, one is merely playing upon words, for a mind which obeys the law of energy is only a portion of the cerebral activities arbitrarily severed from its connections and dubbed "psychic essence," only that this may be forthwith discredited. Energy can only be transformed qualitatively, not quantitatively. A mind conceived as dualistic, if supposed to obey the law of energy, would have to be transformed completely into some other form of energy. But then it would no longer be dualistic, i. e., no longer essentially different from the brain-activities.

Bethe, Uexkull, and others would require us to hold fast to the physiological method, because it alone is exact and restricts itself to what can be weighed and measured. This, too, is an error which has been refuted from time immemorial. Only pure mathematics is exact, because in its operations it makes use solely of equations of abstract numbers. The concrete natural sciences can never be exact and are as unable to subsist without the inductive method of inference from analogy as a tree without its roots. Bethe and Uexkull do not seem to know that knowledge is merely relative. They demand absolute exactitude and cannot understand that such a thing is impossible. Besides, physiology has no reason to pride itself upon the peculiar exactitude of its methods and results.

Although we know that our whole psychology appears as the activity of our cerebrum in connection with the activities of more subordinate nerve-centers, the senses and the muscles, nevertheless for didactic purposes it may be divided into the psychology of cognition, of feeling and volition. Relatively speaking, this subdivision has an anatomico-physiological basis. Cognition depends, in the first instance, on the elaboration of sense-impressions by the brain; the will represents the psycho- or cerebrofugal resultants of cognition and the feelings together with their final transmission to the muscles. The feelings represent general conditions of excitation of a central nature united with elements of cognition and with cerebrofugal impulses, which are relatively differentiated and refined by the former, but have profound hereditary and phylogenetic origins and are relatively independent. There is a continual interaction of these three groups of brain-activities upon one another. Sense-impressions arouse the attention; this necessitates movements; the latter produce new sense-impressions and call for an active selection among themselves. Both occasion feelings of pleasure and pain and these again call forth movements of defense, flight, or desire, and bring about fresh sense-impressions, etc. Anatomically, at least, the sensory pathways to the brain and their cortical centers are sharply separated from the centers belonging to the volitional pathways to the muscles. Further on in the cerebrum, however, all three regions merge together in many neurons of the cortex.

Within ourselves, moreover, we are able to observe in the three above-mentioned regions all varieties and degrees of so-called psychic dignity, from the simplest reflex to the highest mental manifestations. The feelings and impulses connected with self-preservation (hunger, thirst, fear) and with reproduction (sexual love and its concomitants) represent within us the region of long-inherited, profoundly phyletic, fixed, instinct-life. These instincts are nevertheless partially modified and partly kept within due bounds through the interference of the higher cerebral activities. The enormous mass of brain-substance, which in man stands in no direct relation to the senses and musculature, admits not only of an enormous storing up of impressions and of an infinite variety of motor innervations, but above all, of prodigious combinations of these energies among themselves through their reciprocal activities and the awakening of old, so-called memory images through the agency of new impressions. In contradistinction to the compulsory, regular activities of the profoundly phyletic automatisms, I have used the term "plastic" to designate those combinations and individual adaptations which depend on actual interaction in the activities of the cerebrum. Its loftiest and finest expression is the plastic imagination, both in the province of cognition and in the province of feeling, or in both combined. In the province of the will the finest plastic adaptability, wedded to perseverance and firmness, and especially when united with the imagination, yields that loftiest mental condition which gradually brings to a conclusion during the course of many years decisions that have been long and carefully planned and deeply contemplated. Hence the plastic gift of combination peculiar to genius ranks much higher than any simpler plastic adaptability.

The distinction between automatism and plasticity in brain-activity is, however, only a relative one and one of degree. In the most different instincts which we are able to influence through our cerebrum, i. e., more or less voluntarily, like deglutition, respiration, eating, drinking, the sexual impulse, maternal affection, jealousy, we observe gradations between compulsory heredity and plastic adaptability, yes, even great individual fluctuations according to the intensity of the corresponding hereditary predispositions.

Now it is indisputable that the individual Pithecanthropus or allied being, whose cerebrum was large enough gradually to construct from onomatopœas, interjections and the like, the elements of articulate speech, must thereby have acquired a potent means of exploiting his brain. Man first fully acquired this power through written language. Both developed the abstract concept symbolised by words, as a higher stage in generalisation. All these things give man a colossal advantage, since he is thereby enabled to stand on the shoulders of the written encyclopædia of his predecessors. This is lacking in all animals living at the present time. Hence, if we would compare the human mind with the animal mind, we must turn, not to the poet or the savant, but to the Wedda or at any rate to the illiterate. These people, like children and animals, are very simple and extremely concrete in their thinking. The fact that it is impossible to teach a chimpanzee brain the symbols of language proves only that it is not sufficiently developed for this purpose. But the rudiments are present nevertheless. Of course the "language" of parrots is no language, since it symbolises nothing. On the other hand, some animals possess phyletic, i. e., hereditarily and instinctively fixed cries and gestures, which are as instinctively understood. Such instinctive animal languages are also very widely distributed and highly developed among insects, and have been fixed by heredity for each species. Finally it is possible to develop by training in higher animals a certain mimetic and acoustic conventional language-symbolism, by utilising for this purpose the peculiar dispositions of such species. Thus it is possible to teach a dog to react in a particular manner to certain sounds or signs, but it is impossible to teach a fish or an ant these things. The dog comprehends the sign, not, of course, with the reflections of human understanding, but with the capacity of a dog's brain. And it is, to be sure, even more impossible to teach its young an accomplishment so lofty for its own brain as one which had to be acquired by training, than for the Wedda or even the negro to transmit his acquired culture by his own impulse. Even the impulse to do this is entirely lacking. Nevertheless, every brain that is trained by man is capable of learning and profiting much from the experience of its own individual life. And one discovers on closer examination that even lower animals may become accustomed to some extent to one thing or another, and hence trained, although this does not amount to an understanding of conventional symbols.

In general we may say, therefore, that the central nervous system operates in two ways: *automatically* and *plastically*.

The so-called reflexes and their temporary, purposefully adaptive, but hereditarily stereotyped combinations, which respond always more or less in the same manner to the same stimuli, constitute the paradigm of automatic activities. These have the deceptive appearance of a "machine" owing to the regularity of their operations. But a machine which maintains, constructs, and reproduces itself is not a machine. In order to build such a machine we should have to possess the key of life, i. e., the understanding of the supposed, but by no means demonstrated, mechanics of living protoplasm. Everything points to the conclusion that the instinctive automatisms have been gradually acquired and hereditarily fixed by natural selection and other factors of inheritance. But there are also secondary automatisms or habits which arise through the frequent repetition of plastic activities and are therefore especially characteristic of man's enormous brain-development.

In all the psychic provinces of intellect, feeling, and will, habits follow the constant law of perfection through repetition. Through practice every repeated plastic brain-activity gradually becomes automatic, becomes "second nature," i. e., similar to instinct. Nevertheless instinct is not inherited habit, but phylogenetically inherited intelligence which has gradually become adapted and crystalised by natural selection or by some other means.

Plastic activity manifests itself, in general, in the ability of the nervous system to conform or adapt itself to new and unexpected conditions and also through its faculty of bringing about internally new combinations of neurocyme. Bethe calls this the power of modification. But since, notwithstanding his pretended issue with anthropomorphism, he himself continually proceeds in an anthropomorphic spirit and demands human ratiocination of animals, if they are to be credited with plasticity (power of modification),—he naturally overlooks the fact that the beginnings of plasticity are primordial, that they are in fact already present in the Amœba, which adapts itself to its environment. Nor is this fact to be conjured out of the world by Loeb's word "tropisms."

Automatic and plastic activities, whether simple or complex, are merely relative antitheses. They grade over into each other, e. g., in the formation of habits but also in instincts. In their extreme forms they resemble two terminal branches of a tree, but they may lead to similar results through so-called convergence of the conditions of life (slavery and cattle-keeping among ants and men). The automatic may be more easily derived from the plastic activities than *vice versa*. One thing is established, however: since a tolerably complicated plastic activity admits of many possibilities of adaptation in the individual brain, it requires much more nervous substance, many more neurons, but has more resistances to overcome in order to attain a complicated result. The activities of an Amœba belong therefore rather to the plasticity of living molecules, but not as yet to that of coöperating nerve-elements; as cell-plasticity it should really be designated as "undifferentiated."[1] There are formed in certain animals specially complex automatisms, or instincts, which require relatively little plasticity and few neurons. In others, on the contrary, there remains relatively considerable nerve-substance for individual plasticity, while the instincts are less complicated. Other animals, again, have little besides the lower reflex centers and are extremely poor in both kinds of complex activities. Still others, finally, are rich in both. Strong so-called "hereditary predispositions" or unfinished instincts constitute the phylogenetic transitions between both kinds of activity and are of extraordinarily high development in man.

[1] If I expressly refrain from accepting the premature and unjustifiable identification of cell-life with a "machine," I nevertheless do not share the so-called vitalistic views. It is quite possible that science may sometime be able to produce living protoplasm from inorganic matter. The vital forces have undoubtedly originated from physico-chemical forces. But the ultimate nature of the latter and of the assumed material atoms is, of course, metaphysical, i. e., unknowable.

Spoken and especially written language, moreover, enable man to exploit his brain to a wonderful extent. This leads us to underestimate animals. Both in animals and man the true value of the brain is falsified by training, i. e., artificially heightened. We overestimate the powers of the educated negro and the trained dog and underestimate the powers of the illiterate individual and the wild animal.

I beg your indulgence for this lengthy introduction to my subject, but it seemed necessary that we should come to some understanding concerning the validity of comparative psychology. My further task now consists in demonstrating to you what manner of psychical faculties may be detected in insects. Of course, I shall select in the first place the ants as the insects with which I am most familiar. Let us first examine the brain of these animals.

In order to determine the psychical value of a central nervous system it is necessary, first, to eliminate all the nerve-centers which subserve the lower functions, above the immediate innervation of the muscles and sense-organs as first centers. The volume of such neuron-complexes does not depend on the intricacy of mental work but on the number of muscle-fibres concerned in it, the sensory surfaces, and the reflex apparatus, hence above all things on the size of the animals. Complex instincts already require the intervention of much more plastic work and for this purpose such nerve-centers alone would be inadequate.

A beautiful example of the fact that complex mental combinations require a large nerve-center dominating the sensory and muscular centers is furnished by the brain of the ant. The ant-colony commonly consists of three kinds of individuals: the queen, or female (largest), the workers which are smaller, and the males which are usually larger than the workers. The workers excel in complex instincts and in clearly demonstrable mental powers (memory, plasticity, etc.). These are much less developed in the queens. The males are incredibly stupid, unable to distinguish friends from enemies and incapable of finding their way back to their nest. Nevertheless the latter have very highly developed eyes and antennae, i. e., the two sense-organs which alone are connected with the brain, or supra-oesophageal ganglion and enable them to possess themselves of the females during the nuptial flight. No muscles are innervated by the supra-oesophageal ganglion. These conditions greatly facilitate the comparison of the perceptive organs, i. e., of the brain (*corpora pedunculata*) in the three sexes. This is very large in the worker, much smaller in the female, and almost vestigial in the male, whereas the optic and olfactory lobes are very large in the latter. The cortical portion of the large worker brain is, moreover, extremely rich in cellular elements. In this connection I would request you to glance at the figures and their explanation.

Very recently, to be sure, it has come to be the fashion to underestimate the importance of brain-morphology in psychology and even in nerve-physiology. But fashions, especially such absurd ones as this, should have no influence on true investigation. Of course, we should not expect anatomy to say what it was never intended to say.

In ants, injury to the cerebrum leads to the same results as injury to the brain of the pigeon.

In this place I would refer you for a fuller account of the details of sensation and the psychic peculiarities of insects to my more extended work above mentioned: *Sensations des Insectes.*

It can be demonstrated that insects possess the senses of sight, smell, taste, and touch. The auditory sense is doubtful. Perhaps a sense of touch modified for the perception of delicate vibrations may bear a deceptive resemblance to hearing. A sixth sense has nowhere been shown to occur. A photodermatic sense, modified for light-sensation, must be regarded as a form of the tactile sense. It occurs in many insects. This sense is in no respect of an optic nature. In aquatic insects the olfactory and gustatory senses perhaps grade over into each other somewhat (Nagel), since both perceive chemical substances dissolved in the water.

The visual sense of the facetted eyes is especially adapted for seeing movements, i. e., for perceiving relative changes of position in the retinal image. In flight it is able to localise large spatial areas admirably, but must show less definite contours of the objects than our eyes. The compound eye yields only a single upright image (Exner), the clearness of which increases with the number of facets and the convexity of the eye. Exner succeeded in photographing this image in the fire-fly (Lampyris). As the eyes are immovable the sight of resting objects soon disappears so far as the resting insect is concerned. For this reason resting insects are easily captured when very slowly approached. In flight insects orient themselves in space by means of their compound eyes. Odor, when perceived, merely draws these animals in a particular direction. When the compound eyes are covered, all powers of orientation in the air are lost. Many insects can adapt their eyes for the day or night by a shifting of the pigment. Ants see the ultra-violet with their eyes. Honey-bees and humble-bees can distinguish colors, but obviously in other tones than we do, since they cannot be deceived by artificial flowers of the most skilful workmanship. This may be due, to admixtures of the ultra-violet rays which are invisible to our eyes.

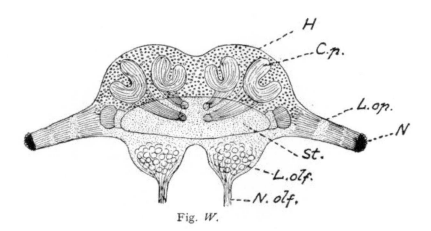

Fig. *W.*

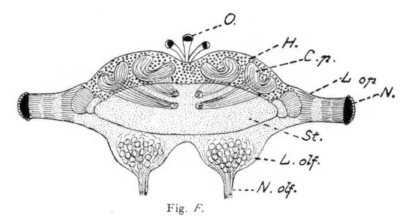

Fig. *F.*]

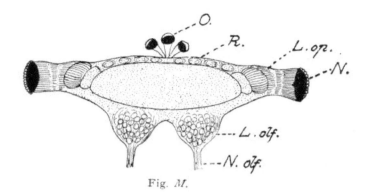

Fig. *M.*

Fig. *M.*

EXPLANATION OF THE FIGURES.

Brain (supra-œsophageal ganglion) of an ant (*Lasius fuliginosus*), magnified 60 diameters, seen from above.

> Fig. *W.* Brain of the Worker.
> Fig. *F.* Brain of the Queen (Female)
> Fig. *M.* Brain of the Male.

St. = Brain trunk. *L. op.* = Lobus opticus (optic lobe). *L. olf.* = Lobus olfactorius sive antennalis (olfactory lobe). *N.* = Facetted eye. *N. olf.* = Nervus olfactorius sive antennalis (olfactory nerve). *O.* = Ocelli, or simple eyes with their nerves (present only in the male and queen). *H.* = Cellular brain cortex (developed only in the worker and queen). *C. p.* = Corpora pedunculata, or fungiform bodies (developed only in the worker and queen). *R.* = Rudimental cortex of male.

The length of the whole ant is:

> in the worker 4.5 mm;
> in the queen 6.0 mm;
> in the male 4.5 mm.

N. B. The striation of the corpora pedunculata and their stems is represented diagrammatically, for the purpose of indicating rather coarsely their extremely delicate fibrillar structure.

The ocelli (simple eyes) play a subordinate rôle, and probably serve as organs of sight for objects situated in the immediate vicinity and in dark cavities.

The olfactory sense has its seat in the antennæ, usually in the club-shaped flagellum, or rather in the pore-plates and olfactory rods of these portions of the antennæ. On account of its external and moveable position at the tip of the antenna, the olfactory organ possesses two properties which are lacking in the vertebrates, and particularly in man. These are:

1. The power of perceiving the chemical nature of a body by direct contact (contact-odor);

2. The power of space-perception and of perceiving the form of objects and that of the animal's own trail by means of odor, and the additional property of leaving associated memories.

The olfactory sense of insects, therefore, gives these animals definite and clear-cut perceptions of space-relations, and enables the animal while moving on the surface of the ground to orient itself with facility. I have designated this sense, which is thus qualitatively, i. e., in its specific energy, very different from our olfactory sense, as the topochemical (olfactory) sense. Probably the pore-plates are used for perceiving odor at a distance and the olfactory rods for contact-odor, but this is pure conjecture. Extirpation of the antennæ destroys the power of distinguishing friends from enemies and deprives the ant of the faculty of orienting itself on the ground and of finding its way, whereas it is possible to cut off three legs and an antenna without seriously impairing these powers. The topochemical sense always permits the ant to distinguish between the directions of its trail, a faculty which Bethe attributes to a mysterious polarisation. The ability to sense different odors varies enormously in different insects. An object possessing odor for one species is often odorless for other species (and for ourselves) and *vice versa*.

The gustatory organs are situated on the mouth-parts. Among insects the reactions of this sense are very similar to our own. Will accustomed some wasps to look in a particular place for honey, which he afterwards mixed with quinine. The wasps detected the substance at once, made gestures of disgust, and never returned to the honey. Mixing the honey with alum had the same result. At first they returned, but after the disagreeable gustatory experience they failed to reappear. Incidentally this is also a proof of their gustatory memory and of their powers of association.

Several organs have been found and described as auditory. But after their removal the supposed reaction to sounds persists. This would seem to indicate that a deceptive resemblance to hearing may be produced by the perception of delicate vibrations through the tactile sense (Dugès).

The tactile sense is everywhere represented by tactile hairs and papillæ. It reacts more especially to delicate tremors of the atmosphere or soil. Certain arthropods, especially the spiders, orient themselves mainly by means of this sense.

It may be demonstrated that insects, according to the species and conditions of life, use their different senses in combination for purposes of orienting themselves and for perceiving the external world. Many species lack eyes and hence also the sense of sight. In others, again, the olfactory sense is obtuse; certain other forms lack the contact-odor sense (e. g., most Diptera).

It has been shown that the superb powers of orientation exhibited by certain aerial animals, like birds (carrier-pigeons), bees, etc., depend on vision and its memories. Movement in the air gives this sense enormous and manifold values. The semi-circular canals of the auditory organ are an apparatus of equilibrium in vertebrates and mediate sensations of acceleration and rotation (Mach-Breuer), but do not give external orientation. For the demonstration of these matters I must refer you to my work above-cited. A specific, magnetic, or other mode of orientation, independent of the known senses, does not exist.

The facts above presented constitute the basis of insect psychology. The social insects are especially favorable objects for study on account of their manifold reciprocal relationships. If in speaking of their behavior I use terms borrowed from human life, I request you, once for all, to bear in mind that these are not to be interpreted in an anthropomorphic but in an analogous sense.

THE PROVINCE OF COGNITION.

Many insects (perhaps all, in a more rudimental condition) possess memory, i. e., they are able to store up sense-impressions in their brains for subsequent use. Insects are not merely attracted directly by sensory stimuli, as Bethe imagines. Huber, myself, Fabre, Lubbock, Wasmann, Von Buttel-Reepen, have demonstrated this fact experimentally. That bees, wasps, etc., can find their way in flight through the air, notwithstanding wind and rain (and hence under circumstances precluding the existence of any possible odoriferous trail), and even after the antennæ have been cut off, to a concealed place where they have found what they desired, though this place may be quite invisible from their nest, and this even after the expiration of days and weeks, is a fact of special importance as proof of the above assertion. It can be shown that these insects recognise objects by means of their colors, their forms, and especially by their position in space. Position they perceive through the mutual relations and succession of the large objects in space, as these are revealed to them in their rapid change of place during flight in their compound eyes (shifting of retinal images). Especially the experiments performed by Von Buttel-Reepen and myself leave no doubt concerning this fact. Additional proof of a different nature is furnished by Von Buttel, who found that ether or chloroform narcosis deprives bees of all memory. By this means enemies can be converted into friends. Under these circumstances, too, all memory of locality is lost and must be reacquired by means of a new flight of orientation. An animal, however, certainly cannot forget without having remembered.

The topochemical antennal sense also furnishes splendid proofs of memory in ants, bees, etc. An ant may perform an arduous journey of thirty meters from her ruined nest, there find a place suitable for building another nest, return, orienting herself by means of her antenna, seize a companion who forthwith rolls herself about her abductrix, and is carried to the newly selected spot. The latter then also finds her way to the original nest, and both each carry back another companion, etc. The memory of the suitable nature of the locality for establishing a new nest must exist in the brain of the first ant or she would not return, laden with a companion, to this very spot. The slave-making ants (*Polyergus*) undertake predatory expeditions, led by a few workers, who for days and weeks previously have been searching the neighborhood for nests of *Formica fusca*. The ants often lose their way, remain standing and hunt about for a long time till one or the other finds the topochemical trail and indicates to the others the direction to be followed by rapidly pushing ahead. Then the pupæ of the *Formica fusca* nest, which they have found, are brought up from the depths of the galleries, appropriated and dragged home, often a distance of forty meters or more. If the plundered nest still contains pupæ, the robbers return on the same or following days and carry off the remainder, but if there are no pupæ left they do not return. How do the Polyergus know whether there are pupæ remaining? It can be demonstrated that smell could not attract them from such a distance, and this is even less possible for sight or any other sense. Memory alone, i. e., the recollection that many pupæ still remain behind in the plundered nest can induce them to return. I have carefully followed a great number of these predatory expeditions.

While Formica species follow their topochemical trail with great difficulty over new roads, they nevertheless know the immediate surroundings of their nest so well that even shovelling away the earth can scarcely disconcert them, and they find their way at once, as Wasmann emphatically states and as I myself have often observed. That this cannot be due to smelling at long range can be demonstrated in another manner, for the olfactory powers of the genus Formica, like those of honey-bees, are not sufficiently acute for this purpose, as has been shown in innumerable experiments by all connoisseurs of these animals. Certain ants can recognise friends even after the expiration of months. In ants and bees there are very complex combinations and mixtures of odors, which Von Buttel has very aptly distinguished as nest-odor, colony- (family-) odor, and individual odor. In ants we have in addition a species-odor, while the queen-odor does not play the same rôle as among bees.

It follows from these and many other considerations that the social Hymenoptera can store up in their brains visual images and topochemical odor-images and combine these to form perceptions or something of a similar nature, and that they can associate such perceptions, even those of different senses, especially sight, odor, and taste, with one another and thereby acquire spatial images.

Huber as well as Von Buttel, Wasmann, and myself have always found that these animals, through frequent repetition of an activity, journey, etc., gain in the certainty and rapidity of the execution of their instincts. Hence they form, very rapidly to be sure, habits. Von Buttel gives splendid examples of these in the robber-bees, i. e., in some of the common honey-bees that have acquired the habit of stealing the honey from the hives of strangers. At first the robbers display some hesitation, though later they become more and more impudent. But he who uses the term habit, must imply secondary automatism and a pre-existing plastic adaptability. Von Buttel adduces an admirable proof of this whole matter and at the same time one of the clearest and simplest refutations of Bethe's innumerable blunders, when he shows that bees that have never flown from the hive, even though they may be older than others that have already flown, are unable to find their way back even from a distance of a few meters, when they are unable to see the hive, whereas old bees know the whole environment, often to a distance of six or seven kilometers.

It results, therefore, from the unanimous observations of all the connoisseurs that sensation, perception, and association, inference, memory and habit follow in the social insects on the whole the same fundamental laws as in the vertebrates and ourselves. Furthermore, attention is surprisingly developed in insects, often taking on an obsessional character and being difficult to divert.

On the other hand, inherited automatism exhibits a colossal preponderance. The above-mentioned faculties are manifested only in an extremely feeble form beyond the confines of the instinct-automatism stereotyped in the species.

An insect is extraordinarily stupid and inadaptable to all things not related to its instincts. Nevertheless I succeeded in teaching a water-beetle (*Dytiscus marginalis*) which in nature feeds only in the water, to eat on my table. While thus feeding, it always executed a clumsy flexor-movement with its fore-legs which brought it over on its back. The insect learned to keep on feeding while on its back, but it would not dispense with this movement, which is adapted to feeding in the water. On the other hand, it always attempted to leap out of the water (no longer fleeing to the bottom of the vessel) when I entered the room, and nibbled at the tip of my finger in the most familiar manner. Now these are certainly plastic variations of instinct. In a similar manner some large Algerian ants which I transplanted to Zurich, learned during the course of the summer months to close the entrance of their nest with pellets of earth, because they were being persecuted and annoyed by our little *Lasius niger*. In Algiers I always saw the nest-opening wide open. There are many similar examples which go to show that these tiny animals can utilise some few of their experiences even when this requires a departure from the usual instincts.

That ants, bees, and wasps are able to exchange communications that are understood, and that they do not merely titillate one another with their antennæ as Bethe maintains, has been demonstrated in so many hundred instances, that it is unnecessary to waste many words on this subject. The observations of a single predatory expedition of Polyergus, with a standing still of the whole army and a seeking for the lost trail, is proof sufficient of the above statement. But, of course, this is not language in the human sense! There are no abstract concepts corresponding to the signs. We are here concerned only with hereditary, instinctively automatic signs. The same is true of their comprehension (pushing with the head, rushing at one another with wide-open mandibles, titillation with the antennæ, stridulatory movement of the abdomen, etc.). Moreover, imitation plays a great rôle. Ants, bees, etc., imitate and follow their companions. Hence it is decidedly erroneous (and in this matter Wasmann, Von Buttel, and myself are of but one opinion) to inject human thought-conception and human ratiocination into this instinct-language, as has been done to some extent, at least, even by Pierre Huber, not to mention others. It is even very doubtful whether a so-called general sensory idea (i. e., a general idea of an object, like the idea "ant," "enemy," "nest," "pupa") can arise in the emmet brain. This is hardly capable of demonstration. Undoubtedly perception and association can be carried on in a very simple way, after the manner of insects, without ever rising to such complex results. At any rate proofs of such an assumption are lacking. But what exists is surely in itself sufficiently interesting and important. It gives us at least an insight into the brain-life of these animals.

Better than any generalisations, a good example will show what I mean.

Plateau had maintained that when Dahlia blossoms are covered with green leaves, bees nevertheless return to them at once. At first he concealed his Dahlias incompletely (i. e., only their ray-florets), afterwards completely, but still in an unsatisfactory manner, and inferred from the results that bees are attracted by odor and not by sight.

a. In a Dahlia bed visited by many bees and comprising about forty-three floral heads of different colors, I covered first seventeen and then eight at 2.15 P. M., September 10th, with grape-leaves bent around them and fastened with pins.

b. Of four I covered only the yellow disc;

c. Of one, on the other hand, I covered only the outer ray-florets, leaving the disc visible.

So many bees were visiting the Dahlias that at times there were two or three to a flower.

Result: Immediately all the completely covered flowers ceased to be visited by the bees. Dahlia (*c*) continued to be visited like those completely visible. The bees often flew to Dahlias (*b*) but at once abandoned them; a few, however, succeeded in finding the disc beneath the leaves.

Then as soon as I removed the covering from a red Dahlia the bees at once flew to it; and soon a poorly concealed specimen was detected and visited. Later an inquisitive bee discovered the entrance to a covered Dahlia from the side or from below. Thenceforth this bee, but only this one, returned to this same covered flower.

Nevertheless several bees seemed to be seeking the Dahlias which had so suddenly disappeared. Towards 5.30 o'clock some of them had detected the covered flowers. Thenceforth these insects were rapidly imitated by the other bees, and in a short time the hidden flowers were again being visited. As soon as a bee had discovered my imposition and found the entrance to a hidden flower, she flew in her subsequent journeys, without hesitation to the concealed opening of the grape-leaf. As long as a bee had merely made the discovery by herself, she remained unnoticed by the others. When this was accomplished by several, however, (usually by four or five,) the others followed their example.

Plateau, therefore, conducted his experiments in a faulty manner and obtained erroneous results. The bees still saw the Dahlias which he at first incompletely concealed. Then, by the time he had covered them up completely, but only from above, they had already detected the fraud and saw the Dahlias also from the side. Plateau had failed to take into consideration the bee's memory and attention.

September 13th I made some crude imitations of Dahlias by sticking the yellow heads of Hieracium (hawkweed) each in a Petunia flower, and placed them among the Dahlias. Neither the Petunias nor the Hieracium had been visited by the bees. Nevertheless many of the honey and humble-bees flew at first to the artefacts in almost as great numbers as to the Dahlias, but at once abandoned the flowers when they had detected the error, obviously by means of their sense of smell. The same results were produced by a Dahlia, the disc of which had been replaced by the disc of a Hieracium.

As a control experiment I had placed a beautiful, odorous Dahlia disc among the white and yellow Chrysanthemums which had been neglected by the bees. For a whole half hour the bees flew by only a few centimeters above the disc without noticing it; not till then was it visited by a bee that happened to be followed by a second. From this moment the Dahlia disc which lay in the path of flight was visited like the others, whereas on the other hand the Petunia-Hieracium artefacts, now known to be fraudulent, were no longer noticed.

Plateau has demonstrated that artificial flowers, no matter how carefully copied from the human standpoint, are not noticed by insects. I placed artefacts of this description among the Dahlias. They remained in fact entirely neglected. Perhaps, as above suggested, the bees are able to distinguish the chlorophyll colors from other artificial hues, owing to admixtures of the ultra-violet rays, or by some other means. But since Plateau imagines that the artificial flowers repel insects, I cut out, Sept. 19th, the following rather crude paper-flowers:

α. A red flower;

β. A white flower;

γ. A blue flower;

δ A blue flower, with a yellow center made from a dead leaf;

ε. A rose-colored piece of paper with a dry Dahlia disc;

ζ. A green Dahlia leaf (unchanged).

It was nine o'clock in the morning. I placed a drop of honey on each of the six artefacts mounted among the Dahlias. For a quarter of an hour many bees flew past, very close to my artefacts but without perceiving and hence without smelling the honey. I went away for an hour. On my return artefact δ was without honey, and must therefore have been discovered by the bees. All the others had remained quite untouched and unnoticed.

With some difficulty I next undertook to bring artefact α very close to a bee resting on a Dahlia. But the attention of the bee was so deeply engrossed by the Dahlia that I had to repeat the experiment four or five times till I succeeded in bringing the honey within reach of her proboscis. The insect at once began to suck up the honey from the paper-flower. I marked the bee's back with blue paint so that I might be able to recognise her, and repeated the experiment with β and ε. In these cases one of the bees was painted yellow, the other white.

Soon the blue bee, which had in the meantime gone to the hive, returned, flew at once to α, first hovering about it dubiously, then to δ, where she fed, then again to α, but not to the Dahlias. Later the yellow bee returned to β and fed, and flew to α and δ where she again fed, but gave as little heed to the Dahlias as did the blue bee.

Thereupon the white bee returned seeking ε, but failing to find it, at once went to feeding on some of the Dahlias. But she tarried only a moment on each Dahlia as if tortured by the *idée fixe* of honey. She returned to the artefacts, the perception of which, however, she was not quite able to associate with the memory of the honey flavor. At last she found a separate piece of ε, which happened to be turned down somewhat behind, and began lapping up the honey.

Thenceforth the three painted bees, and these alone, returned regularly to the artefacts and no longer visited the Dahlias. The fact is of great importance that the painted bees entirely of their own accord, undoubtedly through an instinctive inference from analogy, discovered the other artefacts as soon as their attention had been attracted by the honey on one of them, notwithstanding the fact that the artefacts were some distance from one another and of different colors. For were not the Dahlias, too, which they had previously visited, of different colors? Thus the blue bee flew to α, β, γ, and δ, the yellow to β, α, δ, and γ, the white ε, α, β, and δ. Matters continued thus for half an hour. The hidden green ζ was not found, evidently because it was indistinguishable from the green foliage.

Finally one bee, by herself, having had in all probability her attention attracted by the three others, came to δ and fed. I marked her with carmine. Thereupon she flew to α and drove the blue bee away. Another bee was attracted to ε of her own accord and was painted with cinnobar. Still another bee came by herself to β and was painted green. It was now 12.30 o'clock. The experiment had therefore lasted more than three hours, and during this time only six bees had come to know the artefacts, while the great majority still kept on visiting the Dahlias. But now the other bees began to have their attention attracted by the visitors to the artefacts. One, then two, then three, and finally more new ones followed, and I had not sufficient colors with which to mark them. Every moment I was obliged to replenish the honey. Then I went to dinner and returned at 1.25. At this moment seven bees were feeding on β, two on α, one on γ, three on δ, the white one alone on ε. More than half of all these were new, unpainted followers. Now a veritable swarm of bees threw themselves on the artefacts and licked up the last traces of the honey. Then for the first time, after more than four hours, a bee from the swarm discovered the honey on the artefact ζ, which on account of its color had remained concealed up to this time!

As a pack of hounds throws itself on an empty skeleton, the swarm of bees, now completely diverted from the Dahlias, cast themselves on the completely empty artefacts and vainly searched every corner of them for honey. It was 1.55 P. M. The bees began to scatter and return to the Dahlias. Then I replaced α and β by a red and white paper respectively, which had never come in contact with honey and could not therefore smell of the substance. These pieces of paper, nevertheless, were visited and examined by various bees, whose brains were still possessed with the fixed idea of the flavor of honey. The white bee, e. g., investigated the white paper very carefully for a period of three to four minutes. There could, of course, be no such thing as an unknown force or attraction of odor, or brilliancy of floral colors. This fact can only be explained by an association of space, form, and color memories with memories of taste.

Thereupon I took all the artefacts in my left hand for the purpose of carrying them away. Two or three bees followed me, hovering about my left hand, and tried to alight on the empty artefacts. The space-image had changed and only the color and form could any longer be of service to the bees in their recognition of these objects.

This experiment is so clear and unequivocal that I mention it here among many others. It demonstrates:

1. The space, form, and color perceptions of the honey-bee. That these are possible only through the agency of the compound eyes is proved by other experiments (varnishing the eyes, extirpation of the antennæ, mouth-parts, etc.).

2. The memory of the honey-bee, in particular her visual and gustatory memory.

3. Her power of associating gustatory with visual memories.

4. Her ability instinctively to draw inferences from analogy: If she has once been offered honey in an artefact, she will investigate others, even those of a different color and hitherto unnoticed. These she compares by means of the visual sense, since they are relatively similar, and recognises them as similar

though such objects are most unusual in the bee's experience.

5. Her poor olfactory sense, which is useful only at very close range.

6. The onesidedness and narrow circle of her attention.

7. The rapid formation of habits.

8. The limits of imitation of bees by one another.

Of course, I should not allow myself to draw these conclusions from a single experiment, if they had not been confirmed by innumerable observations by the ablest investigators in this field. Lubbock showed clearly that it is necessary to train a bee for some time to go to a particular color if one wishes to compel her to pay no attention to other colors. This is the only way in which it is possible to demonstrate her ability to distinguish colors. My bees, on the contrary, had been trained on differently colored objects (Dahlias and artefacts) and therefore paid no attention to differences in color. It would be a fallacy to conclude from this that they do not distinguish colors. On the contrary, by means of other experiments I have fully confirmed Lubbock's results.

By 2.20 P. M. all of my bees, even the painted ones, had returned to the Dahlias.

On September 27, a week later, I wished to perform a fresh experiment with the same bees. I intended to make them distinguish between differently colored discs, placed at different points on a long scale, representing on a great sheet of paper, varying intensities of light from white through gray to black. First, I wished to train a bee to a single color. But I had calculated without the bee's memory, which rendered the whole experiment impracticable. Scarcely had I placed my paper with the discs on the lawn near the Dahlia bed, and placed one or two bees on the blue discs and marked them with colors, when they began to investigate all the red, blue, white, black and other discs with or without honey. After a few moments had elapsed, other bees came from the Dahlia bed and in a short time a whole swarm threw itself on the paper discs. Of course, those that had been provided with honey were most visited, because they detained the bees, but even the discs without honey were stormed and scrutinised by bees following one another in their flight. The bees besieged even the paint-box. Among these there was one that I had previously deprived of her antennæ. She had previously partaken of the honey on the blue discs and had returned to the hive. This bee examined the blue piece of paint in the color-box.

In brief, my experiment was impossible, because all the bees still remembered from a former occasion the many-colored artefacts provided with honey, and therefore examined all the paper discs no matter of what color. The association between the taste of the honey and the paper discs had been again aroused by the sight-perception of the latter, and had acquired both consistency and rapid and powerful imitation, because honey happened to be actually found on some of the discs.

Together with the perceptive and associative powers, the power of drawing simple, instinctive inferences from analogy is also apparent. Without this, indeed, the operation of perception and memory would be inconceivable! We have just given an example. I have shown on a former occasion that humble-bees, whose nest I had transferred to my window, when they returned home often confounded other windows of the same façade and examined them for a long time before they discovered the right one. Lubbock reports similar facts. Von Buttel shows that bees that are accustomed to rooms and windows, learn to examine the rooms and windows in other places, i. e., other houses. When Pissot suspended wire netting with meshes twenty-two mm. in diameter in front of a wasp nest, the wasps hesitated at first, then went around the netting by crawling along the ground or avoided it in some other way. But they soon learned to fly directly through the meshes. The sense of sight, observed during flight, is particularly well adapted to experiments of this kind, which cannot therefore be performed with ants. But the latter undoubtedly draw similar inferences from the data derived from their topochemical antennal sense. The discovery of prey or other food on a plant or an object induces these insects to examine similar plants or objects and to perform other actions of a like nature.

There are, on the other hand, certain very stupid insects, like the males of ants, the Diptera and may-flies (Ephemerids) with rudimental brains, incapable of learning anything or of combining sense-impressions to any higher degree than as simple automatisms, and without any demonstrable retention of memory-images. Such insects lead a life almost exclusively dominated by sensory stimuli; but their lives are adapted to extremely simple conditions. In these very instances the difference is most striking, and they demonstrate most clearly through comparison and contrast the *plus* possessed by more intelligent insects.

THE REALM OF WILL.

The notion of volition, in contradistinction to the notion of reflex action, presupposes the expiration of a certain time interval and the operation of mediating and complex brain-activities between the sense-impression and the movement which it conditions. In the operation of the purposeful automatisms of instinct which arouse one another into activity in certain sequences, there is also a time interval, filled out by internal, dynamic brain-processes as in the case of the will. Hence these are not pure reflexes. They may for a time suffer interruption and then be again continued. But their operation is brought about in great measure by a concatenation of complicated reflexes which follow one another in a compulsory order. On this account the term automatism or instinct is justifiable.

If we are to speak of will in the narrower sense, we must be able to establish the existence of individual decisions, which can be directed according to circumstances, i. e., are modifiable, and may, for a certain period, remain dormant in the brain to be still performed notwithstanding. Such volition may be very different from the complex volition of man, which consists of the resultants of prodigiously manifold components that have been long preparing and combining. The ants exhibit positive and negative volitional phenomena, which cannot be mistaken. The ants of the genus Formica Linné are particularly brilliant in this respect, and they also illustrate the individual psychical activities most clearly. The above-mentioned migrations from nest to nest show very beautifully the individual plans of single workers carried out with great tenacity. For hours at a time an ant may try to overcome a multitude of difficulties for the purpose of attaining an aim which she has set herself. This aim is not accurately prescribed by instinct, as the insect may be confronted with several possibilities, so that it often happens that two ants may be working in opposition to each other. This looks like stupidity to the superficial observer. But it is just here that the ant's plasticity reveals itself. For a time the two little animals interfere with each other, but finally they notice the fact, and one of them gives in, goes away, or assists the other.

These conditions are best observed during the building of nests or roads, e. g., in the horse-ant (*Formica rufa*) and still better in *F. pratensis*. It is necessary, however, to follow the behavior of a few ants for hours, if one would have a clear conception of this matter, and for this much patience and much time are necessary. The combats between ants, too, show certain very consistent aims of behavior, especially the struggles which I have called chronic combats (*combats à froid*). After two parties (two colonies brought together) have made peace with each other, one often sees a few individuals persecuting and maltreating certain individuals of the opposite party. They often carry their victims a long distance off, for the purpose of excluding them from the nest. If the ant that has been borne away returns to the nest and is found by her persecutrix, she is again seized and carried away to a still greater distance. In one such case in an artificial nest of a small species of Leptothorax, the persecuting ant succeeded in dragging her victim to the edge of my table. She then stretched out her head and allowed her burden to fall on the floor. This was not chance, for she repeated the performance twice in succession after I had again placed the victim on the table. Among the different individuals of the previously hostile, but now pacified opposition, she had concentrated her antipathy on this particular ant and had tried to make her return to the nest impossible. One must have very strong preconceived opinions if in such and many similar cases one would maintain that ants are lacking in individual decision and execution. Of course, all these things happen within the confines of the instinct-precincts of the species, and the different stages in the execution of a project are instinctive. Moreover, I expressly defend myself against the imputation that I am importing human reflection and abstract concepts into this volition of the ant, though we must honestly admit, nevertheless, that in the accomplishment of our human decisions both hereditary and secondary automatisms are permitted to pass unnoticed. While I am writing these words, my eyes operate with partially hereditary, and my hand with secondary automatisms. But it goes without saying that only a human brain is capable of carrying out my complex innervations and my concomitant abstract reflections. But the ant must, nevertheless, associate and consider somewhat in a concrete way after the manner of an ant, when it pursues one of the above-mentioned aims and combines its instincts with this special object in view. While, however, the instinct of the ant can be combined for only a few slightly different purposes, by means of a small number of plastic adaptations or associations, individually interrupted in their concatenation or *vice versa*, in the thinking human being both inherited and secondary automatisms are only fragments or instruments in the service of an overwhelming, all-controlling, plastic brain-activity. It may be said incidentally that the relative independence of the spinal chord and of subordinate brain-centers in the lower animals (and even in the lower mammals) as compared with the cerebrum, may be explained in a similar manner if they are compared with the profound dependence of these organs and their functions on the massive cerebrum in man and even to some extent in the apes. The cerebrum splits up and controls its automatisms (*divide et impera*).

While success visibly heightens both the audacity and tenacity of the ant-will, it is possible to observe after repeated failure or in consequence of the sudden and unexpected attacks of powerful enemies a form of abulic dejection, which may lead to a neglect of the most important instincts, to cowardly flight, to the devouring or casting away of offspring, to neglect of work, and similar conditions. There is a chronically cumulative discouragement in degenerate ant-colonies and an acute discouragement when a combat is lost. In the latter case one may see troops of large powerful ants fleeing before a single enemy, without even attempting to defend themselves, whereas the latter a few moments previously would have been killed by a few bites from the fleeing individuals. It is remarkable how soon the victor notices and utilises this abulic discouragement. The dejected ants usually rally after the flight and soon take heart and initiative again. But they offer but feeble resistance, e. g., to a renewed attack from the same enemy on the following day. Even an ant's brain does not so soon forget the defeats which it has suffered.

In bitter conflicts between two colonies of nearly equal strength the tenacity of the struggle and with it the will to conquer increases till one of the parties is definitively overpowered. In the realm of will imitation plays a great rôle. Even among ants protervity and dejection are singularly contagious.

THE REALM OF FEELING.

It may perhaps sound ludicrous to speak of feelings in insects. But when we stop to consider how profoundly instinctive and fixed is our human life of feeling, how pronounced are the emotions in our domestic animals, and how closely interwoven with the impulses, we should expect to encounter emotions and feelings in animal psychology. And these may indeed be recognised so clearly that even Uexkuell would have to capitulate if he should come to know them more accurately. We find them already interwoven with the will as we have described it. Most of the emotions of insects are profoundly united to the instincts. Of such a nature is the jealousy of the queen bee when she kills the rival princesses, and the terror of the latter while they are still within their cells; such is the rage of fighting ants, wasps, and bees, the above-mentioned discouragement, the love of the brood, the self-devotion of the worker honey-bees, when they die of hunger while feeding their queen, and many other cases of a similar description. But there are also individual emotions that are not compelled altogether by instinct, e. g., the above-mentioned mania of certain ants for maltreating some of their antagonists. On the other hand, as I have shown, friendly services (feeding), under exceptional circumstances, may call forth feelings of sympathy and finally of partnership, even between ants of different species. Further than this, feelings of sympathy, antipathy, and anger among ants may be intensified by repetition and by the corresponding activities, just as in other animals and man.

The social sense of duty is instinctive in ants, though they exhibit great individual, temporary, and occasional deviations, which betray a certain amount of plasticity.

PSYCHIC CORRELATIONS.

I have rapidly reviewed the three main realms of ant-psychology. It is self-evident that in this matter they no more admit of sharp demarcation from one another than elsewhere. The will consists of centrifugal resultants of sense-impressions and feelings and in turn reacts powerfully on both of these.

It is of considerable interest to observe the antagonism between different perceptions, feelings, and volitions in ants and bees, and the manner in which in these animals the intensely fixed (obsessional) attention may be finally diverted from one thing to another. Here experiment is able to teach us much. While bees are busy foraging on only one species of flower, they overlook everything else, even other flowers. If their attention is diverted by honey offered them directly, although previously overlooked, they have eyes only for the honey. An intense emotion, like the swarming of honey-bees (von Buttel) compels these insects to forget all animosities and even the old maternal hive to which they no longer return. But if the latter happens to be painted blue, and if the swarming is interrupted by taking away the queen, the bees recollect the blue color of their old hive and fly to hives that are painted blue. Two feelings often struggle with each other in bees that are "crying" and without a queen: that of animosity towards strange bees and the desire for a queen. Now if they be given a strange queen by artificial means, they kill or maltreat her, because the former feeling at first predominates. For this reason the apiarist encloses the strange queen in a wire cage. Then the foreign odor annoys the bees less because it is further away and they are unable to persecute the queen. Still they recognise the specific queen-odor and are able to feed her through the bars of the cage. This suffices to pacify the hive. Then the second feeling quickly comes to the front; the workers become rapidly inured to the new odor and after three or four days have elapsed, the queen may be liberated without peril.

It is possible in ants to make the love of sweets struggle with the sense of duty, when enemies are made to attack a colony and honey is placed before the ants streaming forth to defend their nest. I have done this with *Formica pratensis*. At first the ants partook of the honey, but only for an instant. The sense of duty conquered and all of them without exception, hurried forth to battle and most of them to death. In this case a higher decision of instinct was victorious over the lower impulse.

In *résumé* I would lay stress on the following general conclusions:

1. From the standpoint of natural science we are bound to hold fast to the psychophysiological theory of identity (Monism) in contradistinction to dualism, because it alone is in harmony with the facts and with the law of the conservation of energy.

Our mind must be studied simultaneously both directly from within and indirectly from without, through biology and the conditions of its origin. Hence there is such a thing as comparative psychology of other individuals in addition to that of self, and in like manner we are led to a psychology of animals. Inference from analogy, applied with caution, is not only permissible in this science, but obligatory.

2. The senses of insects are our own. Only the auditory sense still remains doubtful, so far as its location and interpretation are concerned. A sixth sense has not yet been shown to exist, and a special sense of direction and orientation is certainly lacking. The vestibular apparatus of vertebrates is merely an organ of equilibration and mediates internal sensations of acceleration, but gives no orientation in space outside of the body. On the other hand the visual and olfactory senses of insects present varieties in the range of their competency and in their specific energies (vision of ultra-violet, functional peculiarities of the facetted eye, topochemical antennal sense and contact-odor).

3. Reflexes, instincts, and plastic, individually adaptive, central nervous activities pass over into one another by gradations. Higher complications of these central or psychic functions correspond to a more complicated apparatus of superordinated neuron-complexes (cerebrum).

4. Without becoming antagonistic, the central nervous activity in the different groups and species of animals complicates itself in two directions: (*a*) through inheritance (natural selection, etc.) of the complex, purposeful automatisms, or instincts; (*b*) through the increasingly manifold possibilities of plastic, individually adaptive activities, in combination with the faculty of gradually developing secondary individual automatisms (habits).

The latter mode requires many more nerve-elements. Through hereditary predispositions (imperfect instincts) of greater or less stability, it presents transitions to the former mode.

5. In social insects the correlation of more developed psychic powers with the volume of the brain may be directly observed.

6. In these animals it is possible to demonstrate the existence of memory, associations of sensory images, perceptions, attention, habits, simple powers of inference from analogy, the utilisation of individual experiences and hence distinct, though feeble, plastic, individual deliberations or adaptations.

7. It is also possible to detect a corresponding, simpler form of volition, i. e., the carrying out of individual decisions in a more or less protracted time-sequence, through different concatenations of instincts; furthermore different kinds of discomfort and pleasure emotions, as well as interactions and antagonisms between these diverse psychic powers.

8. In insect behavior the activity of the attention is one-sided and occupies a prominent place. It narrows the scope of behavior and renders the animal temporarily blind (inattentive) to other sense-impressions.

Thus, however different may be the development of the automatic and plastic, central neurocyme activities in the brains of different animals, it is surely possible, nevertheless, to recognise certain generally valid series of phenomena and their fundamental laws.

Even to-day I am compelled to uphold the seventh thesis which I established in 1877 in my habilitation as *privat-docent* in the University of Munich:

"All the properties of the human mind may be derived from the properties of the animal mind."

I would merely add to this:

"And all the mental attributes of higher animals may be derived from those of lower animals." In other words: The doctrine of evolution is quite as valid in the province of psychology as it is in all the other provinces of organic life. Notwithstanding all the differences presented by animal organisms and the conditions of their existence, the psychic functions of the nerve-elements seem nevertheless, everywhere to be in accord with certain fundamental laws, even in the cases where this would be least expected on account of the magnitude of the differences.

APPENDIX.
THE PECULIARITIES OF THE OLFACTORY SENSE IN INSECTS.

Our sense of smell, like our sense of taste, is a chemical sense. But while the latter reacts only to substances dissolved in liquids and with but few (about five) different principal qualities, the olfactory sense reacts with innumerable qualities to particles of the most diverse substances dissolved in the atmosphere. Even to our relatively degenerate human olfactories, the number of these odor-qualities seems to be almost infinite.

In insects that live in the air and on the earth the sense of taste seems to be located, not only like our own, in the mouth-parts, but also to exhibit the same qualities and the corresponding reactions. At any rate it is easy to show that these animals are usually very fond of sweet, and dislike bitter things, and that they perceive these two properties only after having tasted of the respective substances. F. Will, in particular, has published good experiments on this subject.

In aquatic insects the conditions are more complicated. Nagel, who studied them more closely, shows how difficult it is in these cases to distinguish smell from taste, since substances dissolved in water are more or less clearly perceived or discerned from a distance by both senses and sought or avoided in consequence. Nagel, at any rate, succeeded in showing that the palpi, which are of less importance in terrestrial insects, have an important function in aquatic forms.

In this place we are concerned with an investigation of the sense of smell in terrestrial insects. Its seat has been proved to be in the antennæ. A less important adjunct to these organs is located, as Nagel and Wasmann have shown, in the palpi. In the antennæ it is usually the club or foliaceous or otherwise formed dilatations which accommodate the cellular ganglion of the antennary nerve. I shall not discuss the histological structure of the nerve-terminations but refer instead to Hicks, Leydig, Hauser, my own investigations and the other pertinent literature, especially to K. Kraepelin's excellent work. I would merely emphasise the following points:

1. All the olfactory papillæ of the antennæ are transformed, hair-like pore-canals.

2. All of these present a cellular dilatation just in front of the nerve-termination.

3. Tactile hairs are found on the antennæ together with the olfactory papillæ.

4. The character and form of the nerve-terminations are highly variable, but they may be reduced to three principal types: pore-plates, olfactory rods, and olfactory hairs. The two latter are often nearly or quite indistinguishable from each other. The nerve-termination is always covered with a cuticula which may be never so delicate.

Other end-organs of the Hymenopteran antenna described by Hicks and myself, are still entirely obscure, so far as their function is concerned, but they can have nothing to do with the sense of smell, since they are absent in insects with a delicate sense of smell (wasps) and occur in great numbers in the honey-bees, which have obtuse olfactories.

That the antennæ and not the nerve-terminations of the mouth and palate function, as organs of smell, has been demonstrated by my control experiments, which leave absolutely no grounds for doubt and have, moreover, been corroborated on all sides. Terrestrial insects can discern chemical substances at a distance by means of their antennæ only. But in touch, too, these organs are most important and the palpi only to a subordinate extent, namely in mastication. The antennæ enable the insect to perceive the chemical nature of bodies and in particular, to recognise and distinguish plants, other animals and food, except in so far as the visual and gustatory senses are concerned in these activities. These two senses may be readily eliminated, however, since the latter functions only during feeding and the former can be removed by varnishing the eyes or by other means. Many insects, too, are blind and find their way about exclusively by means of their antennæ. This is the case, e. g., with many predatory ants of the genus Eciton.

But I will here assume these questions to be known and answered, nor will I indulge in polemics with Bethe and his associates concerning the propriety of designating the chemical antennal sense as "smell." I have discussed this matter elsewhere.[2] What I wish to investigate in this place is the psychological quality of the antennal olfactory sense, how it results in part from observation and in part from the too little heeded correlative laws of the psychological exploitation of each sense in accordance with its structure. I assume as known the doctrines of specific energies and adequate stimuli, together with the more recent investigations on the still undifferentiated senses, like photodermatism and the like, and would refer, moreover, to Helmholtz's *Die Thatsachen in der Wahrnehmung*, 1879. Hirschwald, Berlin.

2 "Sensations des Insectes," *Rivista di Biologia Generale*. Como, 1900-1901. For the remainder see also A. Forel, *Mitth. des Münchener entom. Vereins*, 1878, and *Recueil. Zool. Suisse*, 1886-1887.

When in our own human subjective psychology, which alone is known to us directly, we investigate the manner in which we interpret our sensations, we happen upon a peculiar fact to which especially Herbert Spencer has called attention. We find that so-called perceptions consist, as is well known, of sensations which are bound together sometimes firmly, sometimes more loosely. The more intimately the sensations are bound together to form a whole, the easier it is for us to recall in our memory the whole from a part. Thus, e. g., it is easy for me to form an idea from the thought of the head of an acquaintance as to the remainder of his body. In the same manner the first note of a melody or the first verse of a poem brings back the remainder of either. But the thought of an odor of violets, a sensation of hunger, or a stomach-ache, are incapable of recalling in me either simultaneous or subsequent odors or feelings.

These latter conditions call up in my consciousness much more easily certain associated visual, tactile, or auditory images (e. g., the visual image of a violet, a table set for a meal). As ideas they are commonly to be represented in consciousness only with considerable difficulty, and sometimes not at all, and they are scarcely capable of association among themselves. We readily observe, moreover, that visual images furnish us mainly with space recollections, auditory images with sequences in time, and tactile images with both, but less perfectly. These are indubitable and well-known facts.

But when we seek for the wherefore of these phenomena, we find the answer in the structure of the particular sense-organ and in its manner of functioning.

It is well known that the eye gives us a very accurate image of the external world on our retina. Colors and forms are there depicted in the most delicate detail, and both the convergence of our two eyes and their movement and accommodation gives us besides the dimensions of depth through stereoscopic vision. Whatever may be still lacking or disturbing is supplied by instinctive inferences acquired by practice, both in memory and direct perception (like the lacunæ of the visual field), or ignored (like the turbidity of the corpus vitreum). But the basis of the visual image is given in the coördinated *tout ensemble* of the retinal stimuli, namely the retinal image.[3] Hence, since the retina furnishes us with such spatial projections, and these in sharp details, or relations, definitely coördinated with one another, the sense of sight gives us knowledge of space. For this reason, also, and solely on this account, we find it so easy to supply through memory by association the missing remnant of a visual spatial image. For this reason, too, the visual sensations are preëminently associative or relational in space, to use Spencer's expression. For the same reason the insane person so readily exhibits hallucinations of complicated spatial images in the visual sphere. This would be impossible in the case of the olfactory sense.

3 It is well known that in this matter the movements of the eyes, the movements of the body and of external objects play an essential part, so that without these the eye would fail to give us any knowledge of space. But I need not discuss this further, since the antennæ of ants are at least quite as moveable and their olfactory sense is even more easily educated in unison with the tactile sense.

Similarly, the organ of Corti in the ear gives us tone or sound scales in accurate time-sequence, and hence also associations of sequence much more perfectly than the other senses. Its associations are thus in the main associations of sequence, because the end-apparatus registers time-sequences in time-intervals and not as space images.

The corresponding cortical receptive areas are capable, in the first instance, merely of registering what is brought to them by the sense-stimuli and these are mainly associated spatial images for sight and tone or sound-sequences for hearing.

Let us consider for a moment how odors strike the mucous membranes of our choanæ. They are wafted towards us as wild mixtures in an airy maelstrom, which brings them to the olfactory terminations without order in the inhaled air or in the mucous of the palate. They come in such a way that there cannot possibly be any spatial association of the different odors in definite relationships. In time they succeed one another slowly and without order, according to the law of the stronger element in the mixture, but without any definite combination. If, after one has been inhaling the odor of violets, the atmosphere gradually becomes charged with more roast meat than violet particles, the odor of roast succeeds that of violet. But nowhere can we perceive anything like a definitely associated sequence, so that neither our ideas of time nor those of space comprise odors that revive one another through association. By much sniffing of the surface of objects we could at most finally succeed in forming a kind of spatial image, but this would be very difficult owing to man's upright posture. Nevertheless it is probable that dogs, hedge-hogs, and similar animals acquire a certain olfactory image by means of sniffing. The same conditions obtain in the sphere of taste and the visceral sensations for the same reasons. None of these senses furnish us with any sharply defined qualitative relations either in space or time. On this account they furnish by themselves no associations, no true perceptions, no memory images, but merely sensations, and these often as mixed sensations, which are vague and capable of being associated only with associative senses. The hallucinations of smell, taste, and of the splanchnic sensations, are not deceptive perceptions, since they cannot have a deceptive resemblance to objects. They are simply paræsthesias or hyperæsthesias, i. e., pathological sensations of an elementary character either without adequate stimulus or inadequate to the stimulus.

The tactile sense furnishes us with a gross perception of space and of definite relations, and may, therefore, give rise to hallucinations, or false perceptions of objects. By better training its associative powers in the blind may be intensified. The visual sensations are usually associated with tactile localisations.

Thus we see that there is a law according to which the psychology of a sense depends not only on its specific energy but also on the manner in which it is able to transmit to the brain the relations of its qualities in space and time. On this depends the knowledge we acquire concerning time and space relations through a particular sense and hence also its ability to form perceptions and associations in the brain. More or less experience is, of course, to be added or subtracted, but this is merely capable of enriching the knowledge of its possessor according to the measure of the relations of the particular sense-stimuli in space and time.

I would beg you to hold fast to what I have said and then to picture to yourselves an olfactory sense, i. e., a chemical sense effective at a distance and like our sense of smell, capable of receiving impressions from particles of the most diverse substances diffused through the atmosphere, located not in your nostrils, but on your hands. For of such a nature is the position of the olfactory sense on the antennal club of the ant.

Now imagine your olfactory hands in continual vibration, touching all objects to the right and to the left as you walk along, thereby rapidly locating the position of all odoriferous objects as you approach or recede from them, and perceiving the surfaces both simultaneously and successively as parts of objects differing in odor and position. It is clear from the very outset that such sense-organs would enable you to construct a veritable odor-chart of the path you had traversed and one of double significance:

1. A clear contact-odor chart, restricted, to be sure, to the immediate environment and giving the accurate odor-form of the objects touched (round odors, rectangular odors, elongate odors, etc.) and further hard and soft odors in combination with the tactile sensations.

2. A less definite chart which, however, has orienting value for a certain distance, and produces emanations which we may picture to ourselves like the red gas of bromine which we can actually see.

If we have demonstrated that ants perceive chemical qualities through their antennæ both from contact and from a distance, then the antennæ must give them knowledge of space, if the above formulated law is true, and concerning this there can be little doubt. This must be true even from the fact that the two antennæ simultaneously perceive different and differently odoriferous portions of space.[4]

4 It is not without interest to compare these facts with Condillac's discussion (*Treatise on the Sensations*) concerning his hypothetical statue. Condillac shows that our sense of smell is of itself incapable of giving us space knowledge. But it is different in the case of the topochemical sense of smell in combination with the antennary

movements. Here Condillac's conditions of the gustatory sense are fulfilled.

They must therefore also transmit perceptions and topographically associated memories concerning a path thus touched and smelled. Both the trail of the ants themselves and the surrounding objects must leave in their brains a chemical (odor-) space-form with different, more or less definitely circumscribed qualities, i. e., an odor-image of immediate space, and this must render associated memories possible. Thus an ant must perceive the forms of its trail by means of smell. This is impossible, at least for the majority of the species, by means of the eyes. If this is true, an ant will always be able, no matter where she may be placed on her trail, to perceive what is to the right, left, behind or before her, and consequently what direction she is to take, according to whether she is bound for home, or in the opposite direction to a tree infested with Aphides, or the like.

Singularly enough, I had established this latter fact in my "Études Myrmécologiques en 1886" (*Annales de la Societé Entomologique de Belgique*) before I had arrived at its theoretical interpretation. But I was at once led by this discovery in the same work to the interpretation just given. Without knowing of my work in this connection, A. Bethe has recently established (discovered, as he supposes) this same fact, and has designated it as "polarisation of the ant-trail." He regards this as the expression of a mysterious, inexplicable force, or polarisation. As we have seen, the matter is not only no enigma, but on the contrary, a necessary psychological postulate. We should rather find the absence of this faculty incomprehensible.

But everything I have just said presupposes a receptive brain. The formation of lasting perceptions and associations cannot take place without an organ capable of fixing the sense-impressions and of combining them among themselves. Experience shows that the immediate sensory centers are inadequate to the performance of this task. Though undoubtedly receptive, they are, nevertheless, incapable of utilising what has been received in the development of more complex instincts and can turn it to account only in the grosser, simpler reflexes and automatisms. To be sure, a male ant has better eyes than a worker ant, and probably quite as good antennæ, but he is unable to remember what he has seen and is especially incapable of associating it in the form of a trail-image, because he is almost devoid of a brain. For this reason he is unable to find his way back to the nest. On the other hand, it is well known that the brain of a man who has lost a limb or whose hearing is defective, will enable him to paint pictures with his foot, write with the stump of an arm or construct grand combinations from the images of defective senses.

I venture, therefore, to designate as topochemical the olfactory antennal sense of honey-bees, humble-bees, wasps, etc.

Can we generalise to such an extent as to apply this term without further investigation to all arthropods? To a considerable extent this must be denied.

In fact, the multiformity in the structure and development of the arthropod sense-organs is enormous, and we must exercise caution in making premature generalisations.

It is certain that in some aerial insects the olfactory sense has dwindled to a minimum, e. g., in those species in which the male recognises and follows the female exclusively by means of the eyes, as in the Odonata (dragon-flies). To insects with such habits an olfactory sense would be almost superfluous. Here, too, the antennæ have dwindled to diminutive dimensions.

But there are insects whose antennæ are immovable and quite unable to touch objects. This is the case in most Diptera (flies). Still these antennæ are often highly developed and present striking dilatations densely beset with olfactory papillæ. By experiment I have demonstrated the existence of an olfactory sense in such Dipteran antennæ, and I have been able to show that, e. g., in *Sarcophaga vivipara* and other carrion flies, the egg-laying instinct is absolutely dependent on the sensation of the odor of carrion and the presence of the antennæ. In these cases the contact-odor sense is undoubtedly absent. More or less of a topochemical odor-sense at long range must, of course, be present, since the antennæ are external, but the precision of the spatial image must be very imperfect, owing to the immobility of the antennæ. Nevertheless, flies move about so rapidly in the air that they must be able by means of their antennæ to distinguish very quickly the direction from which odors are being wafted. These insects do, in fact, find the concealed source of odors with great assurance. But this is no great art, for even we ourselves are able to do the same by sniffing or going to and fro. But the flies find their way through the air with their eyes and not at all by means of their sense of smell. Hence their olfactory powers probably constitute a closer psychological approximation to those of mammals than to the topochemical odor-sense of ants, for they can hardly furnish any constant and definite space-relations.

Even in many insects with movable antennæ and of less ærial habits, e. g., the chafers and bombycid moths, the antennal olfactory sense is evidently much better adapted to function at a distance, i. e., to the perception of odors from distant objects, than to the perception of space and trails. Such insects find their way by means of their eyes, but fly in the direction whence their antennæ perceive an odor that is being sought.

A genuine topochemical antennal sense is, therefore, probably best developed in all arthropods, whose antennæ are not only movable in the atmosphere, but adapted to feeling of objects. In these cases the still imperfect topochemical odor-sense for distances can be momentarily controlled by the contact-odor-sense and definitively fixed topographically, i. e., topochemically, as we see so extensively practised in the ants.

It would be possible to meet this view with the objection that a contact-odor sense could not accomplish much more than the tactile sense. I have made this objection to myself. But in the first place it is necessary to reckon with the facts. Now it is a fact that insects in touching objects with their antennæ mainly perceive and distinguish the chemical constitution of the objects touched and heed these very much more than they do the mechanical impacts also perceived at the same time. Secondly, the tactile sense gives only resistance and through this, form. On the other hand, the multiplicity of odors is enormous, and it is possible to demonstrate, as I have done for the ants, and Von Buttel-Reepen for the bees, that these animals in distinguishing their different nest-mates and their enemies, betray nothing beyond the perception of extremely delicate and numerous gradations in the qualities of odors.

In combination with topochemical space-perception, these numerous odor-qualities must constitute a spatial sense which is vastly superior to the tactile sense. The whole biology of the social Hymenoptera furnishes the objective proof of this assertion.

It would certainly be well worth while to investigate this matter in other groups of arthropods which possess complex instincts.

In conclusion I will cite an example, which I have myself observed, for the purpose of illustrating the capacity of the topochemical olfactory sense.

The American genus Eciton comprises predatory ants that build temporary nests from which they undertake expeditions for the purpose of preying on all kinds of insects. The Ecitons follow one another in files, like geese, and are very quick to detect new hunting grounds. As "ants of visitation," like the Africo-Indian species of Dorylus, they often take possession of human dwellings, ferret about in all the crevices of the walls and rooms for spiders, roaches, mice, and even rats, attack and tear to pieces all such vermin in the course of a few hours and then carry the booty home. They can convert a mouse into a clean skeleton. They also attack other ants and plunder their nests.

Now all the workers of the African species of Dorylus and of many of the species of Eciton are totally blind, so that they must orient themselves exclusively by means of their antennal sense.

In 1899 at Faisons, North Carolina, I was fortunate enough to find a temporary nest of the totally blind little *Eciton carolinense* in a rotten log. I placed the ants in a bag and made them the subject of some observations. The Eciton workers carry their elongate larvæ in their jaws and extending back between their legs in such a position that the antennæ have full play in front.

Their ability to follow one another and to find their way about rapidly and unanimously in new territory without a single ant going astray, is incredible. I threw a handful of Ecitons with their young into a strange garden in Washington, i. e., after a long railway journey and far away from their nest. Without losing a moment's time, the little animals began to form in files which were fully organised in five minutes. Tapping the ground continually with their antennæ, they took up their larvæ and moved away in order, reconnoitering the territory in all directions. Not a pebble, not a crevice, not a plant was left unnoticed or overlooked. The place best suited for concealing their young was very soon found, whereas most of our European ants under such conditions, i. e., in a completely unknown locality, would probably have consumed at least an hour in accomplishing the same result. The order and dispatch with which such a procession is formed in the midst of a totally strange locality is almost fabulous. I repeated the experiment in two localities, both times with the same result. The antennæ of the Ecitons are highly developed, and it is obvious that their brain is instinctively adapted to such rapid orientation in strange places.

In Colombia, to be sure, I had had opportunities of observing, not the temporary nests, but the predatory expeditions of larger Ecitons (*E. Burchelli* and *hamatum*) possessing eyes. But these in no respect surpassed the completely blind *E. carolinense* in their power of orientation and of keeping together in files. As soon as an ant perceives that she is not being followed, she turns back and follows the others. But the marvellous fact is the certainty of this recognition, the quickness and readiness with which the animals recognise their topochemical trail without hesitation. There is none of the groping about and wandering to and fro exhibited by most of our ants. Our species of Tapinoma and Polyergus alone exhibit a similar but less perfect condition. It is especially interesting, however, to watch the *perpetuum mobile* of the antennæ of the Ecitons, the lively manner in which these are kept titillating the earth, all objects, and their companions.

All this could never be accomplished by a tactile sense alone. Nor could it be brought about by an olfactory sense which furnished no spatial associations. As soon as an Eciton is deprived of its two antennæ it is utterly lost, like any other ant under the same circumstances. It is absolutely unable to orient itself further or to recognise its companions.

In combination with the powerful development of the cerebrum (*corpora pedunculata*) the topochemical olfactory sense of the antennæ constitutes the key to ant psychology. Feeling obliged to treat of the latter in the preceding lecture, I found it necessary here to discuss in detail this particular matter which is so often misunderstood.

[In his latest *Souvenirs entomologiques* (Seventh Series) J. H. Fabre has recorded a number of ingenious experiments showing the ability of the males of Saturnia and Bombyx to find their females at great distances and in concealment. He tried in vain (which was to have been foreseen) to conceal the female by odors which are strong even to our olfactories. The males came notwithstanding. He established the following facts: (1) Even an adverse wind does not prevent the males from finding their way; (2) if the box containing the female is loosely closed, the males come nevertheless; (3) if it is hermetically closed (e. g., with wadding or soldered) they no longer come; (4) the female must have settled for some time on a particular spot before the males come; (5) if the female is then suddenly placed under a wire netting or a bell-jar, though still clearly visible, *the males nevertheless do not fly to her, but pass on to the spot where she had previously rested and left her odor*; (6) the experiment of cutting off the antennæ proves very little. The males without antennæ do not, of course, come again; but even the other males usually come only once: their lives are too short and too soon exhausted.

At first Fabre did not wish to believe in smell, but he was compelled finally, as a result of his own experiments, to eliminate sight and hearing. Now he makes a bold hypothesis: the olfactory sense of insects has two energies, one (ours), which reacts to dissolved chemical particles, and another which receives "physical odor-waves," similar to the waves of light and sound. He already foresees how science will provide us with a "radiography of odors" (after the pattern of the Roentgen rays). But his own results, enumerated above under (4) and (5) contradict this view. The great distances from which the Bombyx males can discern their females is a proof to him that this cannot be due to dissolved chemical particles. And these same animals smell the female only after a certain time and smell the spot where she had rested, instead of the female when she is taken away! This, however, would be inconceivable on the theory of a physical wave-sense, while it agrees very well with that of an extremely delicate, chemical olfactory sense.

It is a fact that insects very frequently fail to notice odors which we perceive as intense, and even while these are present, detect odors which are imperceptible to our olfactories. We must explain this as due to the fact that the olfactory papillæ of different species of animals are especially adapted to perceiving very different substances. All biological observations favor this view, and our psycho-chemical theories will have to make due allowance for the fact.]

Biology, Evolution, Etc.

CHARLES DARWIN, 1809-1882
From a private photograph taken in Darwin's prime.

Darwin and After Darwin

An Exposition of the Darwinian Theory and a Discussion of Post-Darwinian Questions. By GEORGE JOHN ROMANES, LL. D., F. R. S.

Part I. The Darwinian Theory

Pp. xiv., 460. 125 illustrations. Second Edition. With portrait of Darwin. Cloth, $2.00.

"A brilliantly written work."—Review of Reviews.

"The best single volume on the general subject since Darwin's time."—American Naturalist.

"The most lucid and masterly presentation of the Darwinian theory yet written."—Public Opinion.

"The best modern handbook of evolution."—The Nation.

Part II. Post-Darwinian Questions. Heredity and Utility

Pp. xii., 344. With portrait of Romanes. Cloth, $1.50.

"The clearest and simplest book that has appeared in the sphere of the problems it discusses."—Chicago Dial.

"Contains the ripest results of deep study of the evolutionary problem.... No student of the subject can afford to neglect this last volume of Romanes."—Bibliotheca Sacra.

Part III. Post-Darwinian Questions Isolation and Physiological Selection

Pp. 181. With portrait of Mr. Gulick. Cloth, $1.00.

The three volumes of "Darwin and After Darwin" supplied to one order $4.00 net.

AUGUST WEISMANN
Professor in the University of Freiburg in Breisgau.
(Born January 17, 1834.)

Darwinism Illustrated

(Reprint of illustrations from Darwin and After Darwin, Part I.)

Wood engravings explanatory of the Theory of Evolution, selected by and drawn under the direction of Prof. G. J. Romanes. Designed for use in class and home instruction. Pp. 94. Paper, $1.00.

An Examination of Weismannism

By GEORGE JOHN ROMANES. With Portrait of Weismann, and a Glossary of Scientific Terms. Thoroughly indexed. Pp. ix., 221. Cloth, $1.00 net.

"The best criticism of the subject in our language."—The Outlook, N. Y.

"The reader of this work will appreciate from this discussion, better than from the writings of Weismann himself, the significance of the final position adopted by Weismann."—Science.

E. D. COPE. 1840-1897.
"One of the Great Men of Science of the World."
—Science,New York, Sept., 1896.

The Primary Factors of Organic Evolution

By E. D. COPE. 121 illustrations. Pp. 550. Tables, bibliography and index. Cloth, net, $2.00. (10s.).

A comprehensive handbook of the Neo-Lamarckian theory of Evolution, drawing its main evidence from paleontology, as distinguished from œcology (Darwin) and embryology (Weismann). Discusses the "Energy of Evolution," and lays special emphasis on the function of consciousness in organic development.

"Will stand as the most concise and complete exposition of the doctrines of the Neo-Lamarckian school hitherto published. A most valuable text-book for teachers and students."—Science, N. Y.

"A work of unusual originality. No one can read the book without admiring the intimate knowledge of facts and the great power of generalization which it discloses."—Prof. J. McK. Cattell.

On Germinal Selection

As a Source of Definitely Directed Variation. By AUGUST WEISMANN. Translated by THOMAS J. MCCORMACK. Pp., xii, 61. Paper, 25c. (1s. 6d.).

"Professor Weismann considers this one of the most important of all his contributions on the evolution problem.... important as marking some fundamental changes in Weismann's position."—Science, New York.

"Forms the crown and capsheaf of Weismann's theory of heredity."—Exchange.

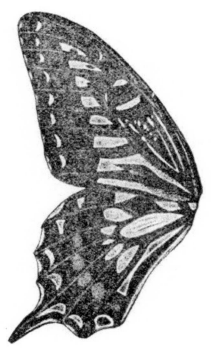

Butterfly's Wing from Eimer's
ORTHOGENESIS.
Illustrating the Definite Character of
Evolution.]

On Orthogenesis (Definite Evolution)

Or the Impotence of Darwinian Selection in the Formation of Species.
By TH. EIMER, Professor of Zoology in the University of Tuebingen.
Translated by THOMAS J. McCORMACK. 19 cuts. Pp., 56. Paper 25c. (1s.
6d.).

This little brochure was written in reply to Weismann's "Germinal
Selection." Prof. Eimer argues upon the same lines as the American Neo-
Lamarckians, Cope, Hyatt, etc. His doctrine of orthogenesis, which he
declares to be a universally valid law, has been framed to show that
organisms develop in definite directions, without regard for utility,
through purely physiological causes, through the transmission of
acquired characters, through the combined agency of the constitution of

48

the animal and the effects of outward influences.

A Mechanico-Physiological Theory of Organic Evolution

Summary. By CARL VON NAEGELI, Translated by V. A. CLARK and F. A. WAUGH, of the University of Vermont. The only original account of Naegeli's theories in English. Pp., 52. Price, paper, 15 cents. (9d.)

Naegeli was the first to propose the general theory of cell-formation accepted to-day. The present little brochure, which is a synopsis of his great work on evolution, will render his difficult theories accessible to English-speaking students, to whom they have hitherto been almost a sealed book.

THE GRASPING POWER OF INFANTS. (From Shute's ORGANIC EVOLUTION.)

A First Book in Organic Evolution

An Introduction to the Study of the Development Theory by D. KERFOOT SHUTE, M.D., Professor of Anatomy in the Medical Department of the Columbian University, Member of the Association of American Anatomists, Member of the Washington Microscopical Society, etc. Pages, xvi—285, 39 illustrations—9 in natural colors. Price, cloth, $2.00 net (7s, 6d. net).

"It is a presentation of the subject for the general reader which is masterly, clear, and entertaining. A profound subject is thoroughly grasped; a technical subject is made plain; and a complex subject is made simple. I am especially delighted with it as a book for auxiliary reading in the High Schools and Colleges of the country."—Major J. W. Powell, Smithsonian Institution, Washington, D. C.

The Principles of Bacteriology

By Dr. FERDINAND HUEPPE, Professor of Hygiene in the University of Prague. Translated from the German and annotated by EDWIN O. JORDAN, Ph.D., Professor in the University of Chicago. 28 cuts. Five colored plates. Pages, 465—x. Price, $1.75 net (9s.). Invaluable to the physician, the scientist, the student of hygiene, and practical people in all walks of life.

"It affords more ground for serious thought and reflection than perhaps any of the works on bacteriology hitherto published. The original and able manner in which the author attacks biological problems of great difficulty and complexity deserves all praise, and we can cordially recommend the book, not only to bacteriologists pure and simple, but also to those physicians who recognize the limitations of medical science."—Nature.

Articles Published in The Monist and The Open Court on Subjects Related to Biology and Evolution

For prices on the back numbers of "The Open Court" and "The Monist," containing the articles here listed, please consult 2nd cover page of this catalogue.

A. R. Wallace on Physiological Selection. By PROF. GEORGE J. ROMANES. "The Monist," Vol. I, No. 1. 50 cents.

On the Material Relations of Sex in Human Society. By PROF. E. D. COPE. "The Monist," Vol. I, No. 1. 50 cents.

The Immortality of Infusoria. By DR. ALFRED BINET. "The Monist," Vol. I, No. 1. 50 cents.

For prices on the back numbers of "The Open Court" and "The Monist," containing the articles here listed, please consult 2nd cover page of this catalogue.

JOSEPH LE CONTE.
(1823-1901.)

The Factors of Evolution. By JOSEPH LE CONTE. "The Monist," Vol. I, No. 3. 50 cents.

The Continuity of Evolution. The Science of Language versus The Science of Life, as represented by Prof. F. Max Mueller and Prof. G. J. Romanes. By DR. PAUL CARUS. "The Monist," Vol. II, No. 1. 50 cents.

Mental Evolution. An Old Speculation in a New Light. By PROF. C. LLOYD MORGAN. "The Monist," Vol. II, No. 2. 50 cents.

The Nervous Ganglia of Insects. By DR. ALFRED BINET. "The Monist," Vol. III, No. 1. 50c.

Panpsychism and Panbiotism. By DR. PAUL CARUS. "The Monist," Vol. III, No. 2. 50 cents.

Automatism and Spontaneity. By DR. EDMUND MONTGOMERY. "The Monist," Vol. IV, No. 1. 50 cents.

Dr. Weismann on Heredity and Progress. By PROF. C. LLOYD MORGAN. "The Monist," Vol. IV, No. 1. 50 cents. Regarded by Prof. Weismann as one of the most powerful criticisms of his doctrine.

The Nervous Centre of Flight in Coleoptera. By ALFRED BINET, "The Monist," Vol. IV, No. 1. 50 cents.

The Problem of Woman From a Bio-Sociological Point of View. By. DR. G. FERRERO. "The Monist," Vol. IV, No. 2. 50 cents.

Modern Physiology. By DR. MAX VERWORN, Professor of Physiology in the University of Jena. "The Monist," Vol. IV, No. 3. 50 cents.

Longevity and Death. (A Posthumous Essay.) By the late PROF. GEORGE J. ROMANES. "The Monist," Vol. V, No. 2. 50 cents.

To Be Alive, What is It? By DR. EDMUND MONTGOMERY. "The Monist," Vol. V, No. 2. 50 cents.

Bonnet's Theory of Evolution. By PROF. C. O. WHITMAN. "The Monist," Vol. V, No. 3. 50 cents.

The Theory of Evolution and Social Progress. By PROF. JOSEPH LE CONTE. "The Monist," Vol. V, No. 4. 50 cents.

Naturalism. By PROF. C. LLOYD MORGAN. "The Monist," Vol. VI, No. 1. 50 cents.

From Animal to Man. By PROF. JOSEPH LE CONTE. "The Monist," Vol. VI, No. 3. 50 cents.

Some Points in Intracranial Physics. By DR. JAMES CAPPIE. "The Monist," Vol. VII, No. 3. 50 cents.

PROF. C. LLOYD MORGAN.
(Born February 6, 1852.)

Illustrative Studies In Criminal Anthropology. (1) "La Bête Humaine" and Criminal Anthropology. (2) Psychiatry and Criminal Anthropology. By PROF. CESARE LOMBROSO. "The Monist," Vol. I, No. 2. 50 cents.

On Egg-Structure and the Heredity of Instincts. By PROF. JACQUES LOEB, of the University of Chicago. "The Monist," Vol. VII, No. 4. 50 cents.

PROF. ERNST HAECKEL.
(Born February 16, 1834.)

The Aryans and the Ancient Italians. A Page of Primitive History. By G. SERGI. "The Monist," Vol. VIII, No. 2. 50 cents.

Regressive Phenomena in Evolution. By PROF. CESARE LOMBROSO. "The Monist," Vol. VIII, No. 3. 50 cents.

Assimilation and Heredity. By PROF. JACQUES LOEB, University of Chicago. "The Monist," Vol. VIII, No. 4. 50 cents.

Evolution Evolved. A Philosophical Criticism. By PROF. ALFRED H. LLOYD, University of Michigan. "The Monist," Vol. IX, No. 2. 50 cents.

The Primitive Inhabitants of Europe. By PROF. GIUSEPPE SERGI, University of Rome, Italy. "The Monist," Vol. IX, No. 3. 50 cents.

Vitalism. By PROF. C. LLOYD MORGAN. "The Monist," Vol. IX, No. 2. 50 cents.

Biology and Metaphysics. By Prof. C. Lloyd Morgan. "The Monist," Vol. IX, No. 4. 50 cents.

The Man of Genius. By Prof. Giuseppe Sergi, University of Rome, Italy. "The Monist," Vol. X, No. 1. 50 cents.

The Psychic Life of Micro-Organisms. A Controversy Between Dr. Alfred Binet and Prof. G. J. Romanes. "The Open Court," Nos. 98, 116 and 127. In complete sets only.

On Retrogression in Animal and Vegetable Life. By Prof. August Weismann. "The Open Court," Nos. 105, 107, 108, 109. In complete sets only.

Evolution and Human Progress. By Prof. Joseph Le Conte. "The Open Court," No. 191.

Phylogeny and Ontogeny. By Prof. Ernst Haeckel. From the "Phylogenie." "The Open Court," No. 214.

Instinct and Intelligence in Chicks and Ducklings. By Prof. C. Lloyd Morgan. "The Open Court," No. 348.

The General Phylogeny of the Protista. By Prof. Ernst Haeckel. "The Open Court," No. 391.

The Kingdom of Protista. By Prof. Ernst Haeckel. "The Open Court," No. 394.

The Cellular Soul. By Prof. Ernst Haeckel. From Haeckel's "Phylogenie." "The Open Court," No. 396.

The Phylogeny of the Plant-Soul. By Prof. Ernst Haeckel, From the "Phylogenie." "The Open Court," No. 398.

Epigenesis or Preformation. By Prof. Ernst Haeckel. "The Open Court," No. 405.

10 Cents Per   Copy $1.00 Per Year

The Open Court

An Illustrated Monthly Magazine

Devoted to the Science of Religion, The Religion of Science and the Extension of the Religious Parliament Idea.

Science is slowly but surely transforming the world.

Science is knowledge verified; it is Truth proved; and Truth will always conquer in the end.

The power of Science is irresistible.

Science is the still small voice; it is not profane, it is sacred; it is not human, it is superhuman; Science is a divine revelation.

Convinced of the religious significance of Science, *The Open Court* believes that there is a holiness in scientific truth which is not as yet recognised in its full significance either by scientists or religious leaders. The scientific spirit, if it but be a genuine devotion to Truth, contains a remedy for many ills; it leads the way of conservative progress and comes not to destroy but to fulfil.

The Open Court on the one hand is devoted to the *Science of Religion*; it investigates the religious problems in the domain of philosophy, psychology, and history; and on the other hand advocates the *Religion of Science*. It believes that Science can work out a reform within the Churches that will preserve of religion all that is true, and good, and wholesome.